MARC BROWN

ARTHUR'S
FIRST SLEEPOVER

RED FOX

For the cousins, Katharine, Jonathan,
Hayley, Shea, and Miles, with love

A Red Fox Book

Published by Random House Children's Books
20 Vauxhall Bridge Road, London SW1V 2SA

A division of Random House UK Ltd
London Melbourne Sydney Auckland
Johannesburg and agencies throughout the world

1 3 5 7 9 10 8 6 4 2

First published in the United States of America by
Little, Brown & Company and simultaneously in Canada by
Little, Brown & Company (Canada) Ltd 1994

First published in Great Britain by Red Fox 1998

Printed in Hong Kong

RANDOM HOUSE UK Limited Reg. No. 954009

ISBN 0 09 926315 7

Arthur was getting ready for his first sleepover.

"It isn't until Saturday," called Mother. "Come in and eat your breakfast."

Father laughed while he read the paper.

"Some man in town says he saw a spaceship," he chuckled.

"Probably the same man who thinks he saw Elvis at the shopping mall," joked Mother.

"I don't believe in aliens," said Arthur.

"Well, the *Daily News* does," said D.W., "and they'll pay a lot of money for a picture of one!"

On the way to school, the girls were talking about the
spaceship.

Arthur wanted to talk about his sleepover.

"We can have the sleepover in my tent!" said Arthur.

"You wouldn't catch me out in a tent with these spaceships
landing," said Muffy.

"Bad news," said Buster. "My mom thinks I'm too young for a sleepover. I can't come."

"But you have to," said Arthur. "It's my first sleepover and you're my best friend."

"Why do they call them sleepovers?" said Francine. "No one ever sleeps."

That afternoon Arthur told his mother about Buster's problem.

"Well, I'll see what I can do," said Mother.

Arthur crossed his fingers while she dialled.

Buster's mother did all the talking.

"Yes. No. Of course not," said Mother. "Absolutely. Good talking with you, too. 'Bye."

Mother smiled and nodded.

"Hooray!" cried Arthur.

"Does Buster's mom know about the spaceship?" asked D.W.

"I saw flashing lights from one today."

"I think that was the Pizza Shop sign," said Mother.

On Saturday morning, Arthur was outside making the tent cosy for his sleepover. His family helped too.

"I was thinking," said D.W., "how do we know you're our real parents and not aliens living inside their bodies?"

"Have you brushed your teeth today?" asked Father.

"And tidied up that mess in your room, young lady," said Mother.

"OK, OK," said D.W.

"They sound real to me," said Arthur.

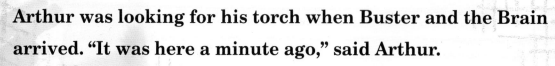

Arthur was looking for his torch when Buster and the Brain arrived. "It was here a minute ago," said Arthur.

"I wonder if you'll see any aliens," said D.W.

"If we do," said the Brain, "how will we communicate with them?"

"Forget the communicating," said D.W. "Take pictures for the *Daily News*! Use my camera. We can split the money."

"Let's make some signs," said Arthur.

"Good idea," said Buster. "But first I have to call my mom."

After they had finished their signs, they unpacked.

"I brought a few snacks," said the Brain.

"I brought a rubber snake," said Arthur, "to keep D.W. away. What did you bring, Buster?"

"Just my collector cards," said Buster, " and my blankie."

"Do you think we really *will* see some aliens tonight?"

"No. Do you?" said Arthur.

"Highly unlikely," said the Brain.

The boys forgot all about aliens.

They were too busy telling jokes and trading cards.

"Pillow fight!" screamed Buster.

"Quiet," said the Brain. "What's that sound?"

"Footsteps," whispered Buster.

And they're getting closer," said Arthur. "Oh! Oh!"

"Pizza delivery," called an unfamiliar voice.

"Compliments of the sleepover parents."

Everyone laughed.

"I almost stopped breathing," said Arthur.

"I almost wet my pants!" said Buster.

Before they knew it, they heard another voice.

"Lights out!" said Father. "It's after nine. Bedtime."

"Already?" said Arthur.

"Thank you for the pizza," said the Brain.

"You're welcome," said Father. "Good night."

"Good night," said the boys sweetly.

As soon as they heard Father go back into the house, they shot out of their sleeping bags like cannonballs.

"I heard bedtime," said the Brain, "but I didn't hear *sleep*time!"

"Let's tell spooky stories," said Arthur.

"How about a game of cards?" suggested Buster.

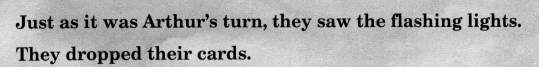

Just as it was Arthur's turn, they saw the flashing lights.

They dropped their cards.

It went very quiet.

"Aliens!" whispered Buster.

"I can't hear any footsteps," whispered Arthur.

"Of course not," said the Brain. "They haven't landed yet."

The lights flashed again.

"They're heading for our tent! Run for your life!"

No one could find the tent flaps.

"Help!" screamed Buster. "Let me out!"

The tent collapsed.

That didn't stop them making a run for it.

But a large maple tree did.

"Ouch!" said Arthur.

"I'm calling my mom," said Buster.

"Look!" said the Brain. "The lights are coming from your house!"

"I think I know this alien," said Arthur. "It's from the planet D.W.!"

Arthur spotted the things they'd used to make the signs. That gave him an idea.

"Let's put our tent back up. I think I know a way we can teach that little space creature a lesson."

Later on, Arthur crept quietly into the house.

D.W. was in her room, laughing.

"What's so funny?" he asked.

"What are you doing up here?" said D.W.

"Did you come in because you were scared?"

"Not really," said Arthur. "I'm returning your camera. You'll probably see an alien before we do."

"I doubt it," said D.W.

"Well, just in case," said Arthur. "Sweet dreams."

Then, very quietly, he returned to his tent.

One minute later, D.W. heard a tap at her window.
"Aliens!" she screamed.
She screamed so loudly it woke up everyone in
the street.
Everyone except Buster, the Brain, and Arthur.
When Mother and Father went out to check on
them, the boys were sleeping like angels.

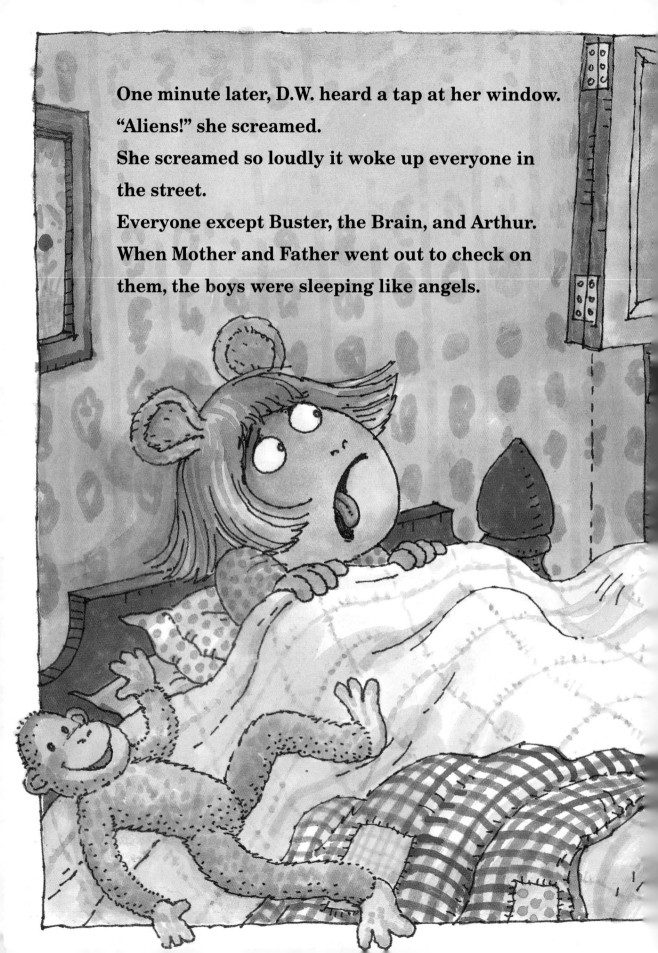

Of course, after Mother and Father went back into the house, it was another story.